VICTOR G. AMBRUS

The Sultan's Bath

HARCOURT BRACE JOVANOVICH, INC., NEW YORK

© Victor G. Ambrus 1971 First published in England by Oxford University Press 1971 First American edition 1972 All rights reserved Printed in Austria ISBN 0-15-282400-6

There was once a Sultan who ruled over a very dry country
where rain hardly ever fell and water was always scarce.
Every day the Sultan sent out his servants to take all the water
they could find in the wells and in the houses for the Sultan's
royal bath.

If there was one thing the Sultan enjoyed, it was his early morning bath. One of his favourite possessions was his toy boat that he floated around in his bath water.

One morning the Sultan jumped into his bath as usual, and hit the bottom hard! All the water, carefully collected for the royal bath, had been stolen overnight. The Sultan flew into a rage and ordered his servants to find the thief immediately.

But though the servants searched the kingdom, they could not find the thief, and the bath water disappeared night after night. Then one night when the moon was bright they caught

Gul-Baba, the gardener, struggling across the courtyard with
two large cans full of the Sultan's bath water.

They followed him, quietly, through a wooden door that led into a small walled garden known only to Gul-Baba. Surrounded by his friends—a peacock, three hedgehogs, some mice, and birds of many kinds—the gardener began to water his plants.

The servants sent for the guard, who dashed into the garden to arrest Gul-Baba. The peacock screamed, the hedgehogs ran under the feet of the guard, the rose-thorns caught at their arms and legs. But it was no use. Gul-Baba was captured and taken away.

He was thrown into a dungeon, where his only companions were three pink-eyed rats and the Sultan's Chief Executioner, who had been put in charge of the prisoner.

The Sultan was surprised to hear of the secret garden and went along to see it for himself. In his dry country flowers were rare, and he was astonished to see so many beautiful plants. Straightaway he sat down under the sunflowers, happier than he had ever been in his life before.

Now no one stole his bath water, and after splashing in his bath, the Sultan went to sit in his garden. But, alas, the flowers soon began to fade, greenfly attacked the roses, and the pea-

cock and the birds and the three little hedgehogs began to droop and hide. The Sultan grew sadder every day. He would not eat, and even his Gypsy band could not cheer him up.

At last he thought to send for Gul-Baba the gardener and explained the matter to him. Now, while Gul-Baba had been in prison, he had been thinking. So he was ready with an answer to the Sultan's problem. If the Sultan would have his bath as usual, Gul-Baba would take the soapy water *after* the bath to use in his garden.

So the Sultan and the gardener came to an agreement. The Sultan would have his bath, Gul–Baba would have the water. The greenfly hated soapy water, but the thirsty plants loved it. Very soon everything was growing again, even the Sultan lending a helping hand.

For the rest of their lives the Sultan and the gardener tended their garden. Everyone was happy, except the Executioner—the Sultan put him in charge of the weeding!